STEAL BACK the MONA LISA!

Meghan McCarthy

Harcourt, Inc. • Orlando Austin New York San Diego Toronto London • Manufactured in China

While Jack is asleep in his room . . .

outside his room, and all the way across the seas in France...

Eiffel Tower →

Louvre ↓

a few crooked crooks are...

Jack was asleep,
but something wakes him up.
Jack has a mission.
But what is it?

QUICK, JACK! GET DRESSED!

Instead of his clothes, Jack finds
nothing but brown suits and brown hats.

He puts on a special-agent watch
that does a very special thing.

Jack struggles out the window.

QUICK, JACK! USE THE LASER LIGHT!

A car is waiting for him outside. A very FAST car.
"I can't drive!" says Jack. "I'm too little."

And they speed away.

Perhaps not.
Jack is being followed.
Will they stop him from saving
the **MONA LISA?**

Hours later, Jack makes it to a plane. But it's not an ordinary plane. It's his own private jet with his own private pilot.

Without wasting a moment, Jack's jacket inflates.
He safely floats to the ground and lands in . . .

RUSSIA!

Jack must find the **MONA LISA**.

But first, he must get his strength back.

"Ah, this drink is good," Jack says to himself.

NO! The juice is poisoned. Jack gets kidnapped and delivered in a truck to a dark, sinister warehouse.

**There, he is made to wear
the most foolish of mustaches . . .**

eat vegetables . . .

**and watch videos of chickens dancing—
OVER and OVER again!**

*AND IT GETS
WORSE....*

He is brought to a very fast boat in an ocean filled
with creatures that look a lot like sharks.

IS THE **MONA LISA** DOOMED?

It sure seems so. And so is Jack!

WITH THE CROOKS GONE, JACK HAS TO ESCAPE!

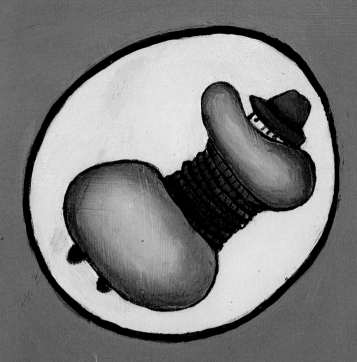

Jack pulls the insta-blimp cord, but that doesn't work.

He tries the laser light, but it only burns a hole in his hat.

He presses the oily-hat button, but that only makes him greasy.

"NOT SO FAST!" shouts Jack.

Then Jack secretly travels to France and makes his way to the Louvre . . .

with something very strange under his jacket.
What could it be?

MISSION ACCOMPLISHED!

Using secret methods too treacherous to mention,
Jack arrives back home, safe and sound in his bed.

And he got away without a mark.....

OR DID HE?

"All the News That's Fit to Paint"

The Mona Lisa Times

International Edition
Paris weather: Some clouds, spotty showers late, watch for burglars and missing paintings.

Vol. CLV...No. 53,409   Today, August 21st   One Euro

© Gianni Dagli Orti/CORBIS

This is a reproduction of the MONA LISA. The real painting is hanging in a museum in Paris called the Louvre. It was painted from 1503 to 1506 by Leonardo da Vinci. He used oil paint on wood.

Perhaps you're wondering just who the real Mona Lisa was? That's what no one knows. Her mysterious, odd smile has intrigued people for centuries. Was she a real person? Was she made up? Some people suspect that she wasn't a woman at all! Did a man pose for this painting?

THE MONA LISA WAS STOLEN!

The MONA LISA is one of the most famous prized paintings in the world. Knowing this, you might think the MONA LISA could never have been stolen. But you'd be wrong!

The theft occurred August 21, 1911. Someone took the painting off the museum wall and waltzed right out of the Louvre with it! Oddly enough, no one noticed it was missing until twenty-four hours later. Sixty inspectors flooded the museum to question visitors and search every nook and cranny for the lost MONA LISA. The Louvre was closed for an entire week.

Who was the thief?

Was it the security guard?   **The cleaning lady?**   **Another painter?**

Inspector Louis Lepine of the Paris police suspected that the thief dressed as a workman and ran out of the museum with the painting under his tunic.

A week later, when the Louvre reopened, thousands of people rushed in to see the empty wall space where the MONA LISA had hung. They couldn't believe her disappearance was possible.

Continued on page A2

Two years went by. Then one day, the MONA LISA reappeared! A man with a dark mustache, who called himself Vincenzo Leonard, visited an antique dealer in Florence, Italy. He showed the dealer the MONA LISA, claiming that he wanted to return the painting to its true home in Italy, where it was first created. All he wanted was a reward: the very large sum of 500,000 lire. The thief, whose real name was Vincenzo Perugia, was soon arrested. It is suspected that Perugia visited the museum the day before the theft and hid there overnight.

Vicenzo Perugia

And the next day, when the museum was closed to visitors, Perugia waited for the security guard to disappear, took the painting off the wall, and snuck out of the building using the service stairs.

Surprisingly, the MONA LISA hadn't traveled far. The painting had been hidden in Perugia's apartment, just blocks from the Louvre!

Today the MONA LISA sits safe and sound behind protective glass. Millions of visitors from all over the world travel to see it every year.

STEAL BACK THE MONA LISA! DEDICATED TO THE TUESDAY-NIGHT LADIES

When a book is due and I need a break, nothing beats a dinner and stories about frozen lizards, iPod cozies, and ¡Mucha Lucha!—M. M.

The illustrations in this book were done with acrylic paints on gessoed paper. The display type was hand painted by Meghan McCarthy. The text type was set in Ed Gothic and Sign Painter.

LIBRARY OF CONGRESS CATALOGING-IN-PUBLICATION DATA

McCarthy, Meghan. Steal back the Mona Lisa!/by Meghan McCarthy. p. cm. Summary: When crooked crooks steal the *Mona Lisa* from the Louvre, Special Agent Jack is sent on a dangerous mission to steal it back. Includes facts about the painting. 1. Leonardo, da Vinci, 1452-1519. *Mona Lisa*—Juvenile fiction. [1. Leonardo, da Vinci, 1452-1519. *Mona Lisa*—Fiction. 2. Crime—Fiction. 3. Spies—Fiction.] I. Title.

PZ7.M4784125Ste 2006
[E]—dc22 2005010552
ISBN-13: 978-0-15-205368-0
ISBN-10: 0-15-205368-9

First edition
A C E G H F D B

Color separations by Colourscan Co. Pte. Ltd., Singapore
Manufactured by South China Printing Company, Ltd., China
This book was printed on totally chlorine-free Stora Enso Matte paper.
Production supervision by Pascha Gerlinger
Designed by Lauren Rille